Shady Character

The shadow crawled across the floor, bleeding forward like thick oil, until it touched the tips of Patrick's feet. He tried to step back, but it was too late. A searing pain suddenly burned through his feet, his knees, and then his waist. His line of sight somehow dropped, as if he were falling through a hole in the floor. He opened his mouth to scream, but nothing came out, and he realized, as the pain reached his chest, that he could no longer scream . . . for he no longer had lungs.

A final thought struck him as his chin touched the burned spot in the floor. But he was gone before he could finish the thought, leaving nothing behind but blue sparks and a black shadow burned into the carpet.

Other X-Files books in this series

The Calusari
Eve
Bad Sign
Our Town
Empathy
Fresh Bones
Control
The Host
Hungry Ghosts

THE X FILES™

Dark Matter

Novelization by Easton Royce

Based on the television series
The X-Files created by
Chris Carter

Based on the teleplay
written by Vince Gilligan

HarperCollins*Entertainment*
An Imprint of HarperCollins*Publishers*

HarperCollins*Entertainment*
An Imprint of HarperCollins*Publishers*
77–85 Fulham Palace Road,
Hammersmith, London W6 8JB

www.**fire**and**water**.com

A Paperback Original 1999
1 3 5 7 9 8 6 4 2

The X-Files™ © Twentieth Century Fox Film Corporation 1999
All rights reserved

A catalogue record for this book
is available from the British Library

ISBN 0 00 648333 X

Set in Goudy

Printed and bound in Great Britain by
Clays Ltd, St Ives plc

All rights reserved. No part of this publication may be
reproduced, stored in a retrieval system, or transmitted,
in any form or by any means, electronic, mechanical,
photocopying, recording or otherwise, without the prior
permission of the publishers.

This book is sold subject to the condition that it shall not,
by way of trade or otherwise, be lent, re-sold, hired out or
otherwise circulated without the publisher's prior consent
in any form of binding or cover other than that in which it
is published and without a similar condition including this
condition being imposed on the subsequent purchaser.

Chapter One

The George Mason Hotel was an oasis of light in the midst of a cold, dark Virginia night. It was the last day of winter—the equinox, on which the darkness of night equally balanced the day. But these chilly nights were a reminder that spring was not as close as the calendar suggested. Behind the gabled windows of the first-class hotel, the wealthy guests went about their business, oblivious to the dark shadows outside.

One such shadow slithered from an alley and headed for the Mason Hotel. Unkempt and unobserved, Chester Banton shielded his eyes from the bright lights of the main entryway, lingering in the shadows. Always lingering in the shadows. Desperation oozed from his pores like a cold sweat.

Mustn't use the front entrance. Too bright. Too bright.

He quickly turned and made his way to the hotel's service entrance, which was deserted at this time of night. One might think him a vampire, the way he cringed from the light and clung to the shadows.

In room 606, Patrick Newirth drew a heavy sigh as he flicked the DO NOT DISTURB sign around the knob and firmly shut the door of his suite. The train ride had rattled his bones and made him ache with weariness. How he despised travel—but his work demanded it. The tobacco industry needed its minions, and Newirth needed his paycheck, regardless of his own disdain for cigarettes. Although his conscience told him to quit the job, his mortgage and the specter of two kids to put through college kept him singing the praises of the tobacco industry as if he really believed them.

Patrick allowed the comfort of the old hotel, his favorite in Richmond, to settle around him like a snug slipper, chasing away his caustic thoughts. Stretching out on the bed, he picked up a pair of reading glasses, poured a drink, and readied himself for a quiet evening.

The elevator door shot open on the sixth floor, and Chester Banton stepped out. Although the hallway was well lit, shadows puddled around lamps that flickered near each door, mimicking the old-time candle flames that had once smoldered in their bronze sconces. The soft gloom blended with sudden pools of brightness, and Banton almost instinctively weaved a serpentine pattern down the hall, avoiding the brightest patches of light.

Just then the lamp on his bedstand flickered, and Patrick gave it an irritated look. Had the world conspired to keep him from relaxing tonight? Apparently so, because now his attention shifted to the sound of someone making his way down the hall. But those footfalls didn't sound right. They didn't sound like the stride of a businessman returning to his hotel suite. Instead they were irregular and sloppy, as if someone was rapidly staggering down the hall.

"Not my business," Patrick mumbled to himself, and forced his attention back to his book . . . until he heard the heavy knocking. At first he thought someone was pounding on his own door—but in a moment he realized it was someone else's. One of the other rooms. Again his reading light flickered and browned out for several telltale heartbeats. That, coupled with the inconsiderate visitor in the hallway, made him feel all the more jittery. Again came the urgent knocking, and then a man's whisper.

"Morris?" the voice said. "Morris, are you there?" And then a pause. Patrick could hear the man's labored breathing and the creaking of the floorboards as he impatiently shifted his weight from one leg to the other. "Morris, I need to talk to you!"

It was too much to bear. Patrick glanced at his phone, wondering if he should call hotel security, but in the end he got up and went to the door.

He put his hand on the doorknob, but rather than turning it, he put his eye to the peephole to scope out the situation. The fisheye lens showed him a shabbily dressed man leaning against the door directly across the hall. The stranger appeared desperate—and weary beyond belief. As Patrick watched, pressed against his own door, the stranger lifted his hand again and pounded even more loudly than before.

"Morris . . . Gail Lambert's dead!" Banton let the sound of his pounding fist echo into silence, and he listened for any sound beyond the door. A thousand thoughts swam through his sleep-deprived mind. *Maybe he's in the bathroom. Maybe he's sleeping. Maybe he's on the phone. Maybe, maybe, maybe.* Everything except: *Maybe he isn't there.* That couldn't be an option. Morris had to be there. He had to listen. He had to help, and he had to do it now. "Morris, please . . ." Banton begged. "Morris, answer me!"

He stopped banging, realizing that at ten P.M.

in a crowded hotel there might be a whole host of guests hearing every word he said. He leaned his face against the door and whispered, with his eyes shut tightly, more like a prayer than anything else. "Morris . . . *please* . . . "

Nothing.

Resigned, he began to back away from the door, for a careless moment ignoring the light shining from the fixture beside him.

Patrick Newirth had long since decided not to open his door and reprimand the desperate man. Instead, he chose to stay silent and watch the late-night drama unfold. Was the man strung out on drugs? Was he demented? Had he said something about someone dying? This little hotel mystery was much more engaging than Patrick's novel, and so he kept his eye glued to the peephole, playing the anonymous voyeur.

As the troubled man stopped pounding and backed away from the door, Patrick thought he felt something. A presence, pressing toward him, making his hair stand on end. He backed away from the peephole, only to see the man's shadow slipping under the large gap beneath his door. As the man backed farther away from the room across the hall, his shadow intruded farther into Patrick's room, bleeding forward like thick oil, until it touched the tips of Patrick's feet.

Patrick tried to step back, but it was too late. He felt scorching blue fire surround him, and his nostrils filled with the acrid stench of ionized, lightning-struck air. Searing pain burned through his feet, his knees, and then his waist. His line of sight had somehow dropped to the doorknob, and still he was dropping, as if through a hole in the floor. He opened his mouth to scream, but nothing came out. He realized as the pain reached his chest that he could no longer scream, for he no longer had lungs.

A final thought struck him as his chin touched the burned spot in the floor. But he was gone before he could finish the thought, leaving nothing but blue sparks and a black shadow.

In the hallway, Chester Banton heard the all-too-familiar sparking. "No!" he shouted, turning on one heel to see his shadow extending across the threshold of the hotel room door. He lunged for the sconce on the wall, reaching in and twisting the burning-hot lightbulb, ignoring the pain in his fingertips as he touched it. Finally the light went out, but he knew it was too late. The sparking had stopped, and the smell began to fill the hallway. The awful smell of incinerated human flesh.

It had happened again.

He had taken every precaution. He had kept away from everyone around him, and yet it had happened again.

Banton stood for a long, anguished moment, watching fingers of smoke escaping from beneath the door of room 606. Then he ran toward the stairs, gasping out sobs of sorrow and terror for a victim he did not even know. As he raced down the long hallway, the many lights flickered and dimmed in his wake. But no matter how fast he ran, his shadow followed close behind.

Chapter Two

The elevator door opened on the sixth floor of the George Mason Hotel. FBI Special Agents Fox Mulder and Dana Scully stepped out, Mulder looking casually down the long hall while Scully stepped purposefully to the left. He followed easily at her side. Although they had been working together for some time now, their differences still marked them more than their similarities. He was sensitive and thoughtful. She was incisive and quick to act. He said what he believed regardless of the consequences, finding intuition his most valuable tool. She weighed her words carefully and believed in few things that couldn't be proved.

Besides their growing friendship, they shared an unwavering enthusiasm for their work.

Scully halted and listened for signs of activity. The message left on her voice mail had said to go to the sixth floor of the George Mason Hotel but hadn't given a room number. Since the incident, the hotel managers had undoubtedly evacuated this floor, both to allow the police an unhampered crime scene and to keep guests from asking too many questions that couldn't be answered.

"Down there," Mulder said, pointing out a thin strip of light spilling into the corridor. Now that Scully was looking at it, she could see that one door along the hallway was cracked open.

"Three apparent abductions in less than a month," Scully said. "According to my contact," she continued, "the Richmond Police Department has hit a dead end. I said we'd come down and have a look."

While Scully was taking this as a simple, straightforward missing persons investigation, Mulder was beginning to sense a deepening intrigue even before they arrived at the crime scene.

Mulder sniffed the air and wondered at the faint smell of smoke. Wasn't this the nonsmoking wing of the hotel? "Who's your contact?" he asked.

"Kelly Ryan. She was one of my students when I was teaching at the academy."

"Burning the midnight oil, isn't she?" He glanced at his watch, noting the late hour, then frowned, thinking again about the unusually bitter smell of smoke.

"She's just been bumped up to detective," Scully explained. "She's nervous about how it would look to her superiors if the FBI got involved."

They stopped by the open door of room 606. A young woman in the room saw them and waved them inside.

"Agent Scully," she said with a breath of intense relief.

Scully reached out and gave her a warm handshake. "Hi, Kelly. This is Agent Mulder."

Mulder leaned over to take her hand also. He could see why Scully had come running when Kelly called. The young woman's tough demeanor only thinly covered her uneasiness. Something was going on here that was clearly out of her realm.

Detective Ryan looked up at Mulder. "Thanks so much for coming, Agent Mulder. I've heard a lot about you." She sent her former teacher an embarrassed look as if she'd said too much.

Mulder hid a grin and leaned over to Scully. "We'll talk later." She grinned back at him. Mulder wandered farther inside the hotel room, considering its neatness and the untouched luggage in the corner. A book lay open on the bed, and a lamp on the nightstand shed a soft light. Everything was in its proper place. No smears of blood on the wall. No signs of a struggle. Nothing seemed to indicate foul play. Scully disappeared into the bathroom. Mulder could hear her opening and shutting the shower door, and then the cupboard under the sink.

"The missing man is Patrick Newirth, age fifty-two," Kelly Ryan said. "A top executive with Morley Tobacco. He was up from Raleigh-

Durham for a meeting. Arrived on an evening train."

Mulder gave the tidy room a puzzled look. The only thing wrong with this picture was that nothing seemed wrong. "How do you know he's missing?"

"He set a wake-up call for six this morning. When the operator tried to place it, there was no answer."

Mulder fingered the book casually. It was opened to page four. "He hadn't read very far."

"Needless to say," Kelly said, "he missed his meeting. They waited three hours before they sent hotel security up. The door was locked, security chain fastened. But when they broke in—no Patrick Newirth."

Mulder drifted to the door and studied the chain. "How about the windows?"

Kelly shook her head and rubbed her neck with frustration. "Locked from the inside. We're six stories up with no fire escape. No way in or out of this room."

"No offense," Mulder said with a slight grin, "but have you checked under the bed?"

Scully walked out of the bathroom at that moment, to give him a dirty look for that question. It only made his grin broaden.

Scully headed for a narrow vent just above the baseboard and knelt down to examine it.

"Agent Scully, what are you looking at?" Kelly asked.

"The heat register," she answered with deadpan exactness.

"You don't think anyone could have squeezed in there?" Kelly said, looking incredulously at the narrow grate.

It seemed to Kelly that nothing wider than a videotape would fit through that.

Scully tested the screws on the grate. "Did your people turn up any forensic evidence?"

"Just this." Kelly headed for the door. She partially closed it, revealing a square of butcher paper the size of a large pizza box. She flipped the paper over and exposed a scorch mark of the same size burned deep into the carpet. It was almost perfectly round, except for some protrusions on one side. Kneeling next to the young police detective,

Mulder examined it. The black, crusted ooze had an organic look, almost like dissolving leather. The smoky smell was stronger here, almost sickly sweet. A familiar scent . . .

"Scully. You see this?" Mulder asked.

Scully hopped up from the heat register and leaned over them. "What is it?"

"We don't know," Kelly said. "The hotel claims it wasn't here before Mr. Newirth checked in. There were similar burns at each of the previous crime scenes."

Scully crouched closer to the scorch mark. "Was Patrick Newirth a smoker?"

"No," Kelly said. "According to his wife, he loathed cigarettes."

"Strange for a man who works for a tobacco company," Scully said wryly.

Mulder straightened up, but his eyes were still glued to the oddly shaped mark. "Did anyone run a test?"

"Yes," Kelly said, professionally. "*I* did."

She rose and walked over to the light, flipping through her notepad. "It's mostly carbon. With some potassium and trace minerals."

Mulder's gaze skidded back to the scorch mark. "Interesting."

"Why?" Kelly asked.

Mulder was too consumed by his evolving hypothesis to answer, so he let Scully answer for him—and was pleased that she knew exactly what he was thinking. "It could be residue from burned human flesh," Scully said.

Giving Kelly a few moments to think, he walked back to the dark blotch and studied it with renewed interest.

"Does this look like an arm to anybody?" Mulder asked.

Scully let out a small sigh. "What are you thinking, Mulder?"

Mulder shook his head, lost in his thoughts. After a moment he stood up.

"This burn mark," he said slowly. "It's right about where I'd be standing if I were answering the door..." He stood over the scorch mark, his feet millimeters away from damaging the evidence. He leaned toward the door. "...and looking out the peephole, isn't it?" He peered out the peephole while Kelly and

Scully watched him uncertainly.

Without waiting for a response, Mulder continued. "And I'd probably only be looking if there was something to look at, right?" He stepped around the puddle of charred ash and reopened the door. He stared into the hallway, still absorbed in his own thoughts.

"That makes sense," Kelly said, and shot Scully a look as if she wondered if it was okay to agree with him. Scully shrugged and waited for Mulder to finish. She had to hear his theory before she could decide whether or not to shoot it down.

Flared sconces lit the hallway with a gentle glow. Except for the one directly across from room 606. Mulder drifted to the unlit sconce. Curious, Scully and Kelly followed him. He studied it for a moment, careful not to touch it.

"Scully," Mulder said. They had worked together for so long that it wasn't necessary for him to say anything further. Scully pulled a latex glove from her pocket and used it to twist the lightbulb further into its socket. The bulb lit.

Mulder nodded as if that confirmed his thinking. "Detective Ryan, can you have this bulb dusted for prints?"

"Of course," she said, puzzled.

"Can you run those against Mr. Newirth's prints, if you have them?" he asked.

"Yes, we got them off his toiletries."

"Can you check those against all hotel employees and registered guests?" Mulder continued. "And do you have the name of the last missing person?"

Kelly flipped through her notepad while Scully unscrewed the lightbulb.

"Margaret Wysnecki was the last missing person," Kelly said.

"Is this your first case, Detective?"

"Yes," Kelly said reluctantly.

Mulder grimaced with understanding. "Any idea why they gave it to you?"

"No one else wanted it," she said. "Because of the lack of evidence, it's still a missing persons case. Not likely to end up on the front page of the daily paper."

"I wouldn't be so sure about that," Mulder said.

"Uh, can I ask?" she said hesitantly. "What do you think may have happened?"

"At first blush?" he said. "Spontaneous human combustion."

As he turned and walked away, Detective Ryan looked at Scully, uncertain of what to make of Mulder's comment.

"You're doing just fine," Scully said as she left.

"Having a little fun?" Scully pounded out of the elevator after her partner. The hotel lobby smelled of leather and wet ferns, a welcome relief after the smoky stench in room 606.

Mulder turned to look at her, debating whether to feign ignorance or not. "How's that?" he asked.

Scully was not fooled. "Spontaneous human combustion?"

Mulder immediately turned serious. Spontaneous human combustion was no laughing matter, and he had his own pet theories about it. "I've got over a dozen case files. A human body is reduced to ashes without any burning or melting. Rapid oxidation without heating."

"Let's forget for the moment that there's no scientific theory to support it."

"Okay," he said with mock amiability, and walked out of the hotel. He stopped short on the sidewalk and stared at the night sky. Scully almost barreled into him but didn't say anything. Her own thoughts churned. How could Patrick Newirth have disappeared from a locked hotel room? What had caused the scorch mark on the carpet? She didn't care if Mulder had a hundred case files on spontaneous human combustion. There had to be a more reasonable explanation.

Chapter Three

The second victim, Margaret Wysnecki, had lived in a small house on a wooded lane in an older section of Richmond. Although the homes were shabby, the yards were raked and the lawns neatly tended. Even in the dark, Scully and Mulder could tell someone was taking care of the house. The sidewalk was swept clean and the mailbox empty. Maybe a relative or a neighbor watched over Margaret's things. It seemed like a street where people looked after their own.

Mulder halted abruptly at a lamppost in the middle of Margaret's tiny yard. The post was heavy black iron, a Victorian antique. On the entire block, Margaret's lamp was the only one not lit.

"What are the odds, huh?" He looked at

Scully and gave her a lopsided grin. "Can you spare another glove?"

Silently she plucked a latex glove out of her pocket and handed it to him. Still troubled by the misshapen circle of ashes on the hotel carpet, she hefted the Wysnecki case file and wondered how similar the marks would be inside Margaret's home. It had been too dark in the car to read the file, so Scully would be going into the house cold. She'd never admit it to Mulder, but she was beginning to get a funny feeling about this case.

Mulder opened the hinged door on the lamp and turned the bulb with the glove, trying to avoid areas from which fingerprints could be lifted. The bulb went on and flooded the yard with light. Scully squinted and saw her own shadow loom large against the flat outlines of the house.

"Darkness covers a multitude of sins," she said wryly.

Mulder unscrewed the lightbulb and the light was quenched again. Holding the bulb between his fingers, he reached inside his coat pocket and pulled out a penlike object.

"Check this out, Scully," he said. "My new tool in the fight against crime. Got it at the local hardware store for forty-nine ninety-five."

With a dramatic flourish, he pointed the tool at the lightbulb and flicked it on. A laser beam sliced through the bulb and backlit the frosted glass, making it glow red. He slowly rotated the bulb until a thumbprint with clearly defined ridges and whorls came into view.

"Neat trick," Scully said. "For your birthday, I'll get you a utility belt."

Wrapping the glove around it, Mulder put the bulb in the inside breast pocket of his coat, and they walked down the unlit path to the front door. Without the yard light, the shadows playing against the front of the house blurred and melted into darker corners. Scully kept her mind focused on what they would find inside while Mulder contemplated the unscrewed lightbulbs.

Scully pushed open the door and fumbled for the light switch. Both blinked for a moment when the entry lamp came on, spilling light onto the foyer and out the door. Scully glanced back outside and saw that the hard light didn't quite reach the lamppost in the yard. Mulder looked down at the carpet and saw . . .

"Scully," he said softly, and touched her arm.

She looked down and saw the fuzzy scorch mark near the front door. This one had no twiglike extrusions; it was a kidney-shaped puddle of char and greasy ooze. Even though she knew that the scene had already been carefully examined by the Richmond Police Department's forensic team, she approached the mark, taking care not to disturb the black residue. Mulder stepped over it casually. Looking around the foyer and front sitting room, he missed nothing. But nothing was what he saw. Just like in room 606. Everything in its place. All tidy and undisturbed. Except for the spot of charred carpet.

Scully opened the case file and read aloud. Mulder listened attentively while riffling through Margaret's unopened mail, which lay on top of an old player piano.

"Margaret Wysnecki, age sixty-six. Widowed, retired from Laramie Tobacco, where she worked in production for thirty-six years. Hey! Tobacco. Patrick Newirth was an executive with Morley Tobacco."

"Yeah," Mulder said. "But half of Richmond earns its paycheck making cancer sticks. It could be just a coincidence."

Scully flipped halfway through the file and nodded. "You're probably right. The first missing person, Gail Lambert, was an engineer. She worked for Polarity Magnetics, Inc."

He nodded absently. He wandered through the sitting room, methodically turning on each lamp. He walked down the hall, turning on an overhead sconce and a night-light set under a plant stand. In the kitchen, he flicked on a battalion of fluorescent rods, which flooded the white tile and avocado-green linoleum with a fearsome glare. Scully followed him, continuing to read the reports. She blinked at the sudden brilliance, but didn't say anything after seeing what Mulder was doing. He was checking for unscrewed bulbs.

Scully found herself counting the fingerprint dustings still shown in sharp relief around the apartment—four on the counter, two on the refrigerator, and eight on the walls, with a partial thrown in for good measure. Mulder inspected a particularly large print near the rooster teapot on the stove and pulled out the bulb to compare. Scully grimaced. It was hard to imagine a killer fire-blasting his victim to cinders, then lingering for a cup of tea.

"Besides Margaret Wysnecki's, they didn't pull any useful prints from here or anywhere else in the house," Scully said. "What makes you think the prints on the lightbulb mean anything?"

"I don't know." Mulder slipped the bulb carefully back into his coat pocket. He continued to examine the stovetop, then the sink, then the long counter. He halted at the trash can near the back door and stepped on the foot pedal.

"Look at this," Mulder said. "Somebody forgot to empty the trash." He happily began to paw through the garbage. From under old bills and newspapers, he pulled out a train ticket.

"'M. Wysnecki,'" he read. "Round trip to Hampton Roads, Virginia. Her return stub is dated March seventeenth."

Scully flipped open the case file again and quickly ran her finger down the top sheet of the report. "March seventeenth. The same day she disappeared." She gave Mulder a meaningful look.

"Patrick Newirth came into town by train, didn't he?" Mulder asked thoughtfully.

She nodded with satisfaction. They had made a possible connection. She leafed through the file, stopped near the middle, and read rapidly.

"Gail Lambert..." Scully pored over the report, then halted, disappointed. "Nope. There's nothing here that puts her anywhere near the Richmond train station the day she disappeared."

"Maybe it was a detail that was overlooked," suggested Mulder.

Scully shrugged. "Even so, what's the significance?"

"Maybe these people aren't just disappearing. Maybe they're being hunted. And the hunter's working the train station."

Scully gave him an astonished look. That was a remarkably sensible deduction for Mulder. "What happened to spontaneous human combustion?"

Mulder shook his head. If Scully was surprised about his reasoning, he was even more so. There were still too many unknowns to be sure of anything. Combustion, yes. "Maybe it was not so spontaneous," Mulder said aloud. "Get on the phone to your young detective and tell her to get a detail down to the train station."

Scully hesitated, wondering if Mulder was jumping the gun. Then she nodded and pulled out her cell phone. While she punched in Kelly's number, the uncomfortable feeling returned. How many more scorch marks before they found their answer?

Chapter Four

The Richmond train station was awash with bleak, diffused light. At least a hundred energy-saving bulbs burned in the greasy, insect-speckled fixtures above. Still, in that huge space, all those lights could not make the place feel any less dreary. They merely chased away the shadows, replacing them with a pale, tinted green glow that matched the olive-drab walls.

Chester Banton sat alone on a long wooden bench. A huge hanging clock in the center of the station displayed the precise time on all four of its sides: ten minutes to twelve midnight. But what did that matter? Every moment of every day felt like midnight to Chester Banton. His life had become a quest for darkness, for light was the enemy now—

the most formidable enemy he, or anyone else, had ever known. He was an unqualified mess. His clothes reeked from days without a shower; his hair was wild and unkempt; and yet, here in this place of abandoned souls, it made him fit in all the more. He seemed little different from the old bag woman who sat on the bench across the way, talking to an imaginary someone beside her. He was just as nameless and faceless as the vagrant who slept slouching in an abandoned shoeshine chair. But he was here for different, and much darker, reasons.

A janitor pushing a cart of mops and pine-scented cleansers clattered by. Banton focused on the speckled linoleum floor tiles as the janitor moved past. Only when he was halfway across the room did Banton look up from the floor and take a deep breath of relief. Yes, there was a reason for being in the train station, a reason that went beyond the need for shelter. But Banton also knew he couldn't stay there all night. To be safe, he had to blend in with the other vagrants, and the others came and went regularly. And so he had to do the same, choosing another place to hide until he could find Morris and end this nightmare once and for all.

Banton stood up from the bench, walking on the cold floor as if on eggshells. He quickly slipped out through a service door, down a flight of stairs, and into an empty alley.

The narrow alley was dimly lit by streetlights high above. As he passed, each lamp dimmed for an instant. He watched as his shadow elongated, died, and was reborn behind him as he moved from one light to another.

Then the light suddenly became harsher. A car had turned down the alley. He looked for a doorway to duck into, but there were only brick walls on either side of him. Then, as the car drew closer, over the glare of its headlights he saw the mounted red-and-blue roof lights. They were turned off, but to him they glared a warning signal all the same. It was a police cruiser. They had found him.

The police car slowed to a halt and an officer casually hopped out, walking toward him with an arrogant swagger.

"Sir, could I speak with you?"

Banton turned and bolted. He didn't know whether this was just some routine questioning or this officer had been sent by a much more sinister government agency, but he knew he didn't want to find out. Either way, this confrontation could only end in misery.

"Hey!" shouted the cop. "Hold on, I just want to ask you a couple of questions."

But Banton had no answers. Not any that the cop would believe. He picked up his pace, splashing though muck-filled puddles until he neared the mouth of the alley. From there he could find a hundred places to hide. But as he neared the alley's end, a second police car turned in and screeched to a halt in front of him. Behind him, the first cop drew his gun. Now Banton was trapped between the stark halogen assault of the cars' headlights. His shadow stretched long and black in two different directions. No! He couldn't let this happen.

"All right!" shouted the cop behind him.

"Stop right there. Don't move, just hold it."

The second cop got out of his cruiser and, taking his lead from the other, drew his gun as well.

Banton swallowed his panic and put his hands where the officers could see them. "Stay...away...from me." He tried to appear calm, reasonable, and rational, but he sounded like a man on the edge of sanity. As the cops approached, he knew he had no other choice. He ran again, this time into the dim shadows of a restaurant's back door.

"Hey! What do you think you're doing?"

He crashed through trash cans and pulled open the screen door, but the back door was locked. He tried the knob again and again, throwing his shoulder against the door, but there was no way he was getting in. He turned to see the cops silhouetted by their headlights. They held their weapons on him, clearly thinking he was dangerous—and rightly so. But they had no idea of just how horribly dangerous he was.

"All right, come out of there!" one of the officers shouted.

"Stay away from me," Banton pleaded. "I don't want to hurt you!"

But the cops only took that as a threat. "Move it!"

With no choice, Banton slowly emerged from the protective darkness around him and stepped into the glare of the headlights. He held his hands out before him and tried once more to reason with the officers.

"Please," he begged. "I'm warning you . . . I'm a dangerous man . . ."

"Keep moving!" the cop to the left shouted. "Out into the light, where we can see you."

Banton took another step forward, two shadows stretching out on either side of him like the wings of a massive beast. Both cops took a step closer. He turned to face the one who had first stopped him.

"No! Please! Don't come any closer!" shouted Banton, watching the tips of their shoes draw nearer to those dark patches of asphalt.

"I want you to lie facedown on the ground," commanded the cop in front of him.

"Now! Down on the ground now!" the other

officer yelled. He took another step closer as Banton backed slowly away.

"Please, don't come any closer!" Banton yelled.

But the cops kept moving toward him from two directions. As Banton inched backward, the cop in back of him stepped into the blackness of his shadow.

"Ahhhh—"

A flash of blue light, a brief cry of pain . . . and the cop was gone, leaving nothing but a black patch, swirling with fading blue light. Even his weapon was gone—fused by the heat of his disintegration into a gray lump at the edge of the organic, black singe.

"Barney!" said the cop behind Banton incredulously. He took a step toward the flickering black patch that had been his fellow officer, and as he did, he brushed against Banton's shadow. The moment contact was made, the shadow leaped out, enveloping the officer's feet, and he, too, quickly dissolved into nothingness.

Banton was once more alone between the two empty police cars, with the residue of two more lives snuffed out of existence.

"No!" Banton screamed, and ran. "Not again!" He didn't know where he was going; all he knew was that he had to get away . . . but he also knew that he could never outrun the darkness.

Chapter Five

Mulder and Scully arrived at the alley behind the train station at dawn, after getting a wake-up call from Kelly Ryan. Two cops had disappeared, the doors of their cars left open and the headlights on, and two more scorch marks had been found on the ground. As he got out of the car, Mulder angled his head toward the street lamp high above him. While he watched it, the light automatically went out in the gray light of morning. In the drizzle, a cluster of people in uniforms and trench coats worked together efficiently. The police and a Richmond forensic team were already busy analyzing the fresh site.

Kelly joined Mulder and Scully and shoved her hands in her pockets to hide their trembling. Scully pretended not to notice. "What happened here, Kelly?" she asked.

"I sent two patrolmen down here last night—just like you told me. We lost radio contact with them around midnight." Her eyes strayed toward the dark marks a few feet away. "All they found this morning were two more scorch marks on the pavement," she said flatly.

Mulder and Scully traded a glance. "Nothing else?" Mulder asked.

Kelly shook her head gravely. "No," she said. "Suddenly this looks like it could be a cop killer case and I'm indirectly responsible." She deliberately did not look toward her superior, Detective Bradley Barron, who watched them closely. Instead, she threw her cold gaze to Mulder, as if her words were an indictment of his hunches.

"You were only doing your job," Scully said firmly.

"Yeah, well, they want to know on what suspicions I sent them down here. And if I tell them I've involved the FBI, they're going to snap."

Mulder frowned. "The prints you pulled off the lightbulb . . ."

Kelly nodded eagerly. She did not want to discuss police politics either. "I ran them against all the hotel staff and guests. Then I ran them through the national databases. No match." She laughed shortly. "Some first case, huh?"

The agents gave her a sympathetic nod, but she didn't see it. Discouraged, Kelly looked glumly at the police tape snapping in the breeze. Scully saw that she didn't look too hopeful. Kelly headed back toward Detective Barron, ducking under the police tape.

"So, these ideas of yours," Scully asked tentatively. "Care to share them?"

Mulder shook his head and stared at the unlit street lamp overhead. "Not yet."

Scully grunted. "You don't have a clue, do you?"

Without taking his eyes off the street lamp, Mulder countered, "He was here, Scully. I was right about that."

They stepped into the car. Things were

beginning to look familiar to both of them—in an unpleasant way. The more they found out, the denser the web of intrigue became, until the bottom seemed to be dropping out of this case.

"All right, where does this leave us?" asked Scully, as she closed the passenger door.

"Maybe with enough to identify the killer," Mulder answered.

"How?"

"He was here last night. He was also probably here on March seventeenth and March thirty-first."

Scully began to zero in on his reasoning. "The days Margaret Wysnecki and Patrick Newirth disappeared."

"Exactly," he answered. "That leaves us with three days of security camera videotapes from the station to cross-reference and find out who this guy really is."

"That assumes we're looking for a guy," Scully said.

Mulder smiled, almost pleased to have been caught by Scully in such a sexist assumption.

"Either way," he said, "the security camera's our only witness."

The train station housed a row of security offices above the terminal. The small video room had a large bank of monitors shoved against the wall, one desk, and little else.

Mulder found himself staring at the light fixture behind the uniformed security officer, a naked bulb with a glare that made his eyes ache. The officer, whose photo badge said BOLEN with no first initial, was polite but not really interested in why Scully and Mulder wanted to see security tapes. He reached for the light switch and the bulb went out. Except where light leaked faintly beneath the curtained windows, the room was plunged into a thick darkness. Troubled, Mulder turned toward the video monitor on the far left, feeling that the hard lights and shadowed darkness meant something crucial to this case.

The video was fuzzy around the edges and gave a wide-angle view of the arrival platform—a strip of concrete crowded with passengers beside a stationary train. After a few moments, a few travelers boarded the train, while the rest hurried out the main exit. According to the time encoded on the tape, it had been about a quarter to midnight.

"It could be any one of these people, Mulder," Scully said. "Or none of them. We've gone through the entire week, and I'm still not sure how you expect to find him."

"That's it for March twenty-second on the arrival deck," the guard interjected. No expression crossed his face.

"Let's go back to the camera inside the terminal," Mulder said. The officer nodded and looked apathetically through the stack of tapes in front of him.

Scully sighed and leaned wearily against the console. "Again?"

"He's got to be on at least one of these tapes," Mulder said. He stared doggedly at the frozen screen. The time and date blinked maddeningly on the corner of the display. On the screen, the bright halogen lamps above the arrival platform cast long stabs of light between the rooted shadows of poles, passengers, and heaped-high packages. The killer could be anyone in this video frame.

"Chances are that he's not carrying around a sign with an arrow," Scully muttered.

The officer slid another tape into the playback machine and cued it to the time they wanted. The screen came to life again, this time showing the uniformly lit terminal interior.

"There you go," the officer said. He scratched his ear and suppressed a yawn.

Mulder and Scully watched the videotape for a few minutes, and it seemed just as ordinary as the first time they'd seen it. A few passengers came and went. A flower vendor closed up shop and waved at a janitor as she walked past. A row of benches was empty except for a few homeless men and one old woman who had come in to escape the chill of the March night.

One of the transients pulled his baseball cap down over his eyes and slid lower on an old shoeshine bench. The old woman nearby gestured and mumbled to no one in particular. On the bench closest to the camera, a man with dark curly hair and a rumpled jacket stood and rotated slowly, staring at the floor. When he'd made a complete circle, he carefully sat down again. Another man with a frayed raincoat that dragged on the floor stood and shuffled toward a vending machine.

Mulder focused on the man with curly hair. There was something strangely familiar about his actions and his appearance. Mulder gestured at the screen. "This guy. See this guy? He's always sitting there."

Scully squinted at the man slumped on the bench. She had dismissed him as a transient. His clothes were worn, and he looked as if he hadn't bathed in weeks. She shot Mulder a questioning look.

"In almost every tape," Mulder said. "Look at what he does here."

The man, his head bowed, stood up from the bench. His gaze never moved from the floor. Turning in another perfect circle, he continued to stare at the ground. Then he sat down again.

Scully frowned at Mulder. "What? Looking at the floor?"

"Yeah." Mulder gave the screen a puzzled look. "Why's he doing that?"

Her eyebrows rose. "Probably the same reason he spends his whole day in a train station."

Mulder leaned over the security officer's shoulder. "Can you stop this and blow it up by two hundred percent?"

Bolen nodded and swallowed another yawn. He froze the screen with one keystroke. After entering in "200," he hit the magnification button. The frozen image of the man increased several times in size.

"Now can you reframe and blow it up again? There's something on his jacket there."

Scully shot Mulder a look of intrigue as the security officer complied. She gave the screen another glance. What did Mulder see about this man that she didn't? To her, the man looked like one of the city's many homeless. Just like the one sitting behind him on another bench. Or the one shuffling down toward the vending machines in the background.

The security officer finished centering the figure and magnified the picture again.

While Bolen and Scully stared at the man's face, Mulder noticed something farther down. A badge on his pocket? Maybe his name? Mulder pointed at the screen for the others. "There. Look." Bolen grunted, then focused and magnified the image again.

On the breast pocket of the man's grubby windbreaker, a grainy insignia popped into view. The circles intersected like the traditional atomic symbol. A name appeared beneath the logo.

"'Polarity Magnetics, Inc.,'" he read.

Mulder felt Scully start with surprise, and he swung around to face her. She looked at him with excitement. "That's where Gail Lambert worked," she explained.

Bingo! They shared a grin and an electric surge of satisfaction while Bolen stared blankly at the screen. Finally—the first break in the case! It couldn't be a coincidence—the man on the screen in front of them *must* be part of this. Killer, victim, or witness? Mulder felt the thrill of the hunt as he narrowed his sights on the suspect before them.

Chapter Six

The building that housed Polarity Magnetics was an unimpressive sky-blue box with smoky windows, reflecting the dreary gray sky. The company sign on an expansive concrete patio showed the atomic insignia with its swirling electrons. It seemed to symbolize a technology company of energetic hopes, but the parking lot with its two lone cars and empty sidewalks didn't exactly match that image.

The two agents got out of their car and stared at the sparse group of saplings in front of the building. Leaves sprouted along the tender branches. After finding this latest break in the case, Scully felt a similar budding of hope. She had wanted to call Kelly from the train station, but decided to wait until they had more to go on. They walked up the sidewalk from the visitor's parking lot to the tinted glass doors.

Mulder rang the bell while Scully peered through the glass. "Looks like it's been closed up," she said. She stepped abruptly back as a face loomed suddenly in front of her. The face in the window exchanged a startled look with Scully.

The door swung open. A bespectacled man in a creased suit regarded them warily. "Yes?"

"We're Agents Mulder and Scully with the FBI," Scully said, flashing her identification. "We're looking for someone who might have worked here." She handed him a photocopied printout of the still frame that showed the suspect at the train station. Still feeling unnerved by his sudden appearance, Scully examined the man curiously. He stared owlishly back at her, and then looked down at the photo.

He stiffened, and his gaze froze on the picture. "I'm Christopher Davey," he said absently, and took another close look at the picture. "Dr. Christopher Davey." He pursed his lips. "When was this taken?" he asked abruptly.

"March twenty-second," Mulder said, his voice quickening with urgency. "Do you know this man?"

Davey, still frowning at the picture, seemed oblivious to Mulder's driving concern. "Sure. I know him. Dr. Chester Banton. He was my business partner."

Scully turned to Mulder and saw that he shared her thoughts. "You mean he's not here anymore?" she asked.

Davey shook his head and gave them an assessing look. Scully knew he'd finally caught on to their grave concern. "This picture is the first I've seen of him in almost five weeks. I wondered if he wasn't going to turn up dead."

"How's that?" Mulder asked, disconcerted.

Davey scratched his head and sighed. "Chester was involved in a terrible accident here."

Accident? Scully exchanged a look with Mulder. Maybe there would be a scientific explanation, after all, for the reports of blue lights and the scorched remains. Davey hesitated as if he was undecided about how much more to tell them. Finally he reluctantly invited them in. "Come with me."

As he led them down the hallway, he launched into an awkward pitch to sell the two FBI agents on projects he'd been developing.

"Polarity Magnetics does"—Dr. Davey faltered and corrected himself—"or *did* primarily two types of research. Mostly we were designing mag-lev applications—high-speed transportation devices like 'people movers,' bullet trains . . . would you like to see a model?" Without waiting for a response, he veered into a lab, stepping casually over a wide rubber strip in the doorway, and flicked on the lights. Mulder gave Scully an impatient look, but Scully shrugged. Maybe the answer to what happened to Dr. Banton would be here.

Inside the lab, Davey busied himself powering up generators, analyzers, and processors. On the floor, a tiny bullet train screamed down a similar track. It moved faster and faster until it became a blur of motion. Scully edged farther into the room and felt the hot wind as the little train passed. This was no child's toy. Davey pressed another button, and a miniature elevator slid quickly and smoothly down the wall. Another button, and a fighter jet shot off its magnetic rails and slammed into the padding on the opposite wall. Scully and Mulder stared wide-eyed as it remained there, lodged tightly, its hull still smoking.

Scully had to raise her voice to be heard over all the racket. "But which of these projects was Dr. Banton working on?"

Davey's shoulders slumped. The strain in his voice that had appeared at the mention of Banton's name returned. "These projects are mainly mine. Chester worked on the initial specifications and some of the simulations, but then he'd lose interest. For him, these were just a way to pay the bills. It was the theoretical stuff he was really interested in."

"What sort of theoretical study was he involved with?" Mulder asked alertly.

"Researching dark matter," Davey said reluctantly. He shut down the power grid. The bullet train screeched to a stop. "Chester was obsessed with quantum particles. You know—neutrinos, gluons, mesons, quarks—that sort of thing."

Scully nodded, her scientific interest piqued. "Subatomic particles."

Davey adjusted his glasses. "The mysteries of the universe. The building blocks of reality."

"Except no one knows if they truly exist," Scully reminded him.

Davey led Mulder and Scully out of the lab and further down the hallway.

"Chester was sure they existed," Davey said, reaching in his pocket for a special card-key. "So sure that he'd bet his life on it," he said with quiet finality.

"This is where it happened," Davey said with a sigh. "Chester was working to isolate a new particle. He'd been working on it for a year."

"This is a particle accelerator?" Scully asked,

impressed. She'd never seen one outside a government lab or a heavily funded university.

Davey nodded. "Designed by Chester himself. One fifth as powerful as the Texas supercollider but in a fraction of the space."

Scully blinked. How could that be possible? Chester would have to be a genius greater than any she'd read about. The best minds in the United States and in Europe hadn't created a particle accelerator that small.

"Powered by what?" Mulder asked, wincing slightly at the powerful energy hum that filled the room.

"A few billion megawatts," Davey said with a grimace. "Virginia Power loved us."

Scully glanced through the porthole again, then eased herself gingerly away from the door. That was an impossible and dangerous amount of power. "*Exactly what* happened?" she asked.

Davey parked himself on a stool and restlessly fingered a spectrum analyzer cable. "The work involved the bombardment of beta particles with an alpha target. Negative against positive. Chester had everything set and had started the countdown when he realized he'd made a mistake. There was something that needed to be readjusted in the target room."

Davey pointed to a video monitor that displayed a picture of the interior of the target room just beyond them.

"Except you can't stop the countdown once you've begun. But Chester didn't want to blow the test. Like I said, it cost a fortune in electricity every time we turned the accelerator on. There was time to safely make the change, but I had left the room for a minute when Chester decided to go in. He didn't realize until it was too late . . . the door had locked behind him."

Scully's eyes met Mulder's, and she knew they were both thinking about that odd rumpled man sitting on the train station bench. How terrified had he been when the hatch slammed shut? Had he called for help? Had he frantically tried to rip that heavy door from its hinges? Had he been only too aware of the fail-safe locks he'd personally designed into this circular tomb and waited for death with cold fear trickling through his veins?

Davey stood with his back to them and shuddered, thinking his own dark thoughts. He then walked to the door of the target room, punched in a numerical code that released the lock, and opened the thick blast door. Scully halted at the red warning sign on the front of the door as she and Mulder approached the small chamber. It read, DANGER! EXTREME HIGH VOLTAGE! DO NOT ENTER IF WARNING LIGHT IS FLASHING!

"Look at this, Scully," Mulder said softly. Scully stepped around him and stared at the charred silhouette of a man burned into the floor and wall. It was almost surreal, Picasso-like. But this wasn't paint. It was black ashes and something else. She leaned a little closer to the wall.

"As far as I can tell, it burned Chester's shadow right into the wall," Davey said from the doorway. Pain deadened his voice.

"How did he survive?" Scully asked under her breath.

Davey heard her. "All I can figure is that the dark matter escaping off the target—Chester—had virtually no mass. It slid right through his body."

"Like getting an X ray," Mulder said wonderingly.

"A two-billion-megawatt X ray." He glanced toward the camera in the corner, and his face was troubled as he remembered the accident. "When I looked up on the monitor and saw what was happening—that Chester was trapped in here—I panicked. I cut the power, but it was too late. I remember looking up and seeing Chester. He was perfectly calm. Almost like he wanted it to happen. Like he was finally going to experience the dark matter he had theorized in some kind of physical way. As if the truth might come into him." The strangeness of Davey's words seemed to strike Mulder with the impact of an epitaph. A final word for a damned soul. Davey lowered his head, and mumbled a choked "Excuse me" as he walked out of the room.

"What do you think?" Mulder asked Scully.

She crouched close to the scorched shadow outline on the wall. She looked at the physical evidence before her. "It's the same material that was found at each crime scene. Maybe what we're dealing with *is* some kind of spontaneous human combustion after all, Mulder." She was just as surprised as he was to hear herself admit it.

Mulder shook his head. "I'm less convinced of that now, Scully."

"Well, what do you think it is?" she asked, surprised by his change.

In the corner of the room, high above Scully's head, a red light blinked on the camera. Slowly it panned down until it pointed right at Scully, but neither of them noticed. . . .

Mulder shrugged. "I don't know. But whatever it is, it's somehow connected to Dr. Chester Banton. Maybe even part of him."

"Well, whatever it is . . . we have to find him."

"There's only one place to start looking," he said.

The camera froze in place as Davey lost sight of the agents' retreating forms on the video monitor he had used to watch their every move inside the target room.

Chapter Seven

It was already dark by the time Mulder and Scully made it back to the train station. They hurried in and quickly split up to thoroughly canvass the entire area: Mulder to the main terminal and Scully to the arrival platform and back alley.

After checking all the corners, even the men's rest room, Mulder returned to the benches where Banton had been sitting in the security tape. Mulder sat in the same spot on the same bench. Trying to reenact Banton's movements, he stared fixedly at the floor in front of him.

A few minutes later, Scully approached him, checking her watch against the wall clock. Mulder didn't look up even when she lightly touched his shoulder.

"No sign of him, Mulder," she said. "Maybe he's moved on." She frowned when Mulder continued to ignore her. "What are you looking at?" she asked curiously.

"In the videotape, Dr. Banton kept staring at the floor." Mulder stood up, still studying the floor. "I'm trying to figure out what he would have been looking at."

"Maybe the exposure affected his mind," she suggested. "Nonsensical, repetitive behavior is a common trait of mental illness."

But Mulder was unconvinced. He stared up at the ceiling, then back at the floor, then back at the ceiling again.

"I called Detective Ryan," Scully said. "She's checking the prints on the lightbulbs against Banton's."

"Hmmm." Mulder returned his attention to the worn floor tiles. "Did you tell her about Dr. Banton's accident?"

Scully shook her head. "I only told her he was a possible suspect. I said it was too early to get her hopes up—there are still too many unanswered questions."

"Like?" he asked without looking up.

"*Like* a motive. *Like* a murder weapon. *Like* a cause of death."

At that, Mulder raised his head and shot Scully a look. Then he dropped his eyes back to the ground.

"Look at this, Scully," said Mulder. "There are hardly any shadows cast."

"What do you mean?"

Mulder stood up and lifted his arm parallel to the floor, but no shadow appeared on the ground. "The lighting here—it's indirect. Soft light. Maybe that's what Dr. Banton was looking for."

Scully cocked her head toward Mulder. "Looking for his shadow?"

Mulder moved his hand back and forth, but still there was no shadow to mirror his movement. "Looking for it," he said. "Or trying to lose it."

Mulder looked up then and saw him. A disheveled man, almost blending in with the homeless who loitered in the corners around them. But he didn't quite blend in, did he?

And he was wearing a Polarity Magnetics jacket.

Mulder gently touched Scully's elbow to get her attention. She looked up and saw Banton, but, like Mulder, she was experienced in dealing with unstable individuals and didn't react. In spite of what they knew, they were confronted by a powerful unknown. And when you're faced with a human unknown, you make no sudden movements.

"Dr. Banton?" said Mulder calmly.

At the sound of his name, apprehension and fear seized Chester Banton. He was like a cornered animal, and just as any cornered animal would react, he tried to escape.

He spun and took off toward the nearest exit, running at full speed.

Banton didn't know who they were, but they knew him, they had called him by name. He couldn't be certain whether they were with the police or the government, but either way, he didn't want to hang around and find out. As he burst through the door, he found himself on the deserted arrival platform, where row after row of trains waited silently for morning commuters. The man and woman who had spotted him were in close pursuit. He looked back only once, and that glance confirmed that these people were as dangerous as he'd thought they were, for they both had pulled weapons from inside their jackets. After seeing that, Banton did not look back again. He took a sharp left turn, so sharp that he banged against the side of one of the stationary trains. In an instant, he found an open door and climbed into the train and out the other side to an adjacent platform. With half a dozen trains and platforms, the station was a maze that he could lose himself in if he took the right turns and ran fast enough. But as he raced along the platform, he heard the telltale sound of running feet. The man who had been chasing him had cut through the train as well, one car in front of him.

"Stop right there!" he shouted at Banton with his weapon raised; but Banton had no intention of stopping. He spun on his heel and headed in the other direction, only to be faced by the redheaded woman, who was pointing her pistol right at his chest. For Banton, it was a horrible replay of the night before, when those two unlucky cops had met their sudden and painful end in the dark alley behind the terminal. He was certain these two would try to apprehend him and would meet the same fate, leaving two more deaths on his hands.

"Dr. Banton," the man said again. Trapped between the two of them, Banton tried to catch his breath.

"Please, just leave me alone," he said. But still they both slowly stalked closer. "Wait!" he shouted as Mulder moved closer. He looked up to see a single station light casting a shadow toward the woman, a shadow much darker than the natural one she cast. Neither of them made a move to lower their weapons.

"We're federal agents, Dr. Banton," the man said.

Banton shook his head. "It doesn't matter! You don't understand, you're making a big mistake. You have to stay away from me." Still they slowly approached. "Wait!" he shouted, as Mulder moved closer. "It will *kill* you. It doesn't care who you are!" The man stopped, but Banton turned to see the woman still creeping forward, her shoes just an inch from the black pitch of his shadow. Banton stood transfixed, knowing that any move now would be futile and that this woman, in a fraction of a second, would be just another shapeless patch of neutrons dissolved into the concrete platform.

BLAM!

Suddenly a shot was fired and the light above his head was blasted out. Without the light, his shadow disappeared into the darkness just as the woman stepped into the spot where it had been. Banton spun on one heel to look at the man, who now fired a second shot at another light farther down the platform, taking that one out as well. A wave of relief washed through Banton with the dying of those lights. "Oh, thank God!" he said.

"We're agents Scully and Mulder, with the FBI," said the woman.

"We're here to help," said the man. They lowered their weapons and moved closer, and for the first time in many weeks, Dr. Chester Banton breathed a sigh of relief.

Chapter Eight

Yaloff Psychiatric Hospital was a maximum-security facility tucked away in Piedmont, Virginia. Many of its wings were reserved for the criminally insane, whose mad ravings could be heard through the cold concrete walls and floors. And then there was the wing reserved for those whose sanity was still in question; a mental way station where people waited to appear in court. A judge would determine whether they were insane and whether their actions were criminal or the actions of a ruined mind. Chester Banton was one of those souls under observation. Scully and Mulder had brought him there themselves, but turned over full credit to Kelly Ryan, since the Richmond Police

Department still had no idea that the FBI was involved with this case.

Scully and Mulder stood outside the steel door of the room, peering in through the narrow window of one-way glass. The light inside the little room was bright. Chester Banton sat there on the hospital-white bed in hospital-gray clothes, staring down at the ground, just as he had done at the train station. Mulder wondered what thoughts played in the tortured scientist's mind, hour after hour, day after day, as he looked down at his own shadow. Mulder turned to the psychiatrist beside him, who had the key to the door. "I thought the orders were to keep this patient in the dark," said Mulder.

"He insisted on soft light," the psychiatrist explained. "It's the only way he would let us open the door." Mulder peered into the room again to see that, indeed, the light shining from the fluorescents up above was filtered through a makeshift diffuser so that no shadows were cast in the room.

The psychiatrist unlocked the door and

pulled open the heavy bolt. The door swung open on its heavy hinges. Banton turned to them as they stepped in, his tired eyes showing no emotion.

Mulder couldn't help flinching slightly as the psychiatrist stepped from the room and closed the door behind them. The door was quickly bolted from the outside, sounding with a metallic echo like the toneless peal of a funeral bell.

I've been in rooms like this before, thought Mulder, *with true psychotics—and very dangerous ones. Why am I so unnerved now?* But he already knew the answer. It was because there was something more in the room than the person of Chester Banton. There was something dark and deadly. And although the soft light kept it at bay, it was still there, waiting for the chance to kill again. Scully took the moment in stride. She maintained a cool professionalism, clearly not letting speculation on "shadows" cloud her judgment.

"We'd like you to explain what happened to those people," Scully said.

Banton looked up from the floor, glancing at the two of them with just the slightest disdain. "How can you even begin to understand what it's like?" he said. "To have lived through what I've lived through?"

Mulder almost took a step closer, but then thought better of it. "We're *trying* to understand," he said.

"Living in a train station day and night," continued Banton, "living like a bum. Afraid to fall asleep because of what might happen."

"The accident in the lab," said Scully, getting right to the point, "the quantum bombardment. You believe that altered you physically?"

Banton let out an ironic little chuckle. "Yeah . . . yeah, you could say that." This time, Mulder did take a step forward.

"Could you tell us how?" As Mulder approached, Banton stood and shuffled away toward a corner of the small room.

"Even if I could," he said, shaking his head, "you wouldn't understand."

"But it had something to do with dark matter," prompted Scully. "Is that correct?"

Banton turned to her with a burning gaze. "It has *everything* to do with dark matter," he said bitterly. Then he softened and his eyes changed from glaring to pleading. Pleading for someone to understand, pleading for someone to believe. "My shadow," he said slowly, "isn't . . . mine. It's like a black hole. It splits molecules into component atoms. It unzips electrons from their orbits; it reduces matter into pure energy."

"So that's how you killed Gail Lambert?" asked Scully. Banton shook his head and held out his hands as if begging for some sort of absolution.

"*That wasn't me*," he insisted. "Gail Anne was my colleague; she was my friend. The night after the accident, I went to see her. I was just standing near her car, looking right at her as she got out"—Banton fixed his eyes on Mulder—"and then she was gone."

Mulder moved closer to him, and again Banton backed away, until he was in the corner. "You have no control over it?" Mulder asked.

"If I had control over it," asked Banton, "do you think I would let it go around killing people? All I can do is study it and try to divine its true nature before *they* do."

"They?" questioned Mulder.

Banton moved away from the corner, getting closer to Mulder. Then, in a hushed tone, as if the walls had a thousand ears, he whispered, "You know—the government." He threw a suspicious glance at Scully, who still kept her distance. "There are agencies out there," he said quietly. "Government agencies that I'm sure you don't know about. They're the ones who are after me, and when they find me, they're gonna do the brain suck they've been just dying to do."

"Brain suck," repeated Mulder flatly. He threw a glance at Scully, who looked up almost involuntarily. So much for her detached professionalism. Mulder turned back to Banton. "And what would be the purpose of this 'brain suck'?"

"The purpose would be to steal what has taken me years to accomplish," said Banton, practically snarling at the thought of it. "And don't think they wouldn't kill to get it." Then he turned and looked away from Mulder again.

"But if they killed you," asked Mulder, "wouldn't your shadow just—"

"—Disappear?" replied Banton, completing Mulder's thought. Banton's eyes seemed to grow older and wearier. "Who knows?" he said helplessly. "That's why you have to get me out of here." He approached Mulder again, speaking even more desperately than before. "If I die, there may be nothing left to tether this thing. It might just run free, destroying everyone in its path."

Suddenly Mulder heard the bolt being thrown and the door swinging open. He turned to see Kelly Ryan.

"I'm sorry," she said, "but I'll have to ask you to discontinue your interrogation of the subject." Her voice was cold and distant, as if Mulder and Scully were total strangers to her. Strangers who were making waves and interfering with the investigation, rather than the ones who had solved it.

Mulder locked eyes with Dr. Banton for a long instant. He wished he could give some reassurance to the physicist, but right now Mulder knew he couldn't promise anything to anyone—not while the Richmond PD was calling the shots. He and Scully left the room with Detective Ryan. The young detective said nothing to them as the door was bolted and they walked down the hall, leaving Dr. Chester Banton behind them locked in his softly lit, shadowless room.

In the hallway, they were met by another man holding a case folder.

"This is Detective Barron," Kelly said stiffly. "He's the primary on this case."

"Yes," Barron said, looking up from the file. "I was wondering what your involvement is here."

Mulder shrugged innocently. "We caught the guy."

"I appreciate that," Barron said. His lips compressed in a tight line. "But no one appears to recall the FBI's being invited in on this case."

"Agent Mulder and I are here strictly in an unofficial capacity," Scully said quickly, using her best damage-control skills.

Barron fixed Scully with a scowl. "Who brought you in?"

Scully saw Kelly give her a beseeching look, but Scully was careful not to glance in her direction. "We were curious about the unexplained nature of the case," she said impersonally.

Barron nodded, but he seemed only half appeased by Scully's explanation. He shot Mulder a suspicious look, then turned back to Scully.

"Banton's prints place him at two of the crime scenes," he said. "And Transit Authority tapes show him in the immediate vicinity of the two most recent victims. So I'd say things are looking pretty much explained."

"Really?" Mulder asked. Scully stiffened slightly. "Have you talked to Dr. Banton?" Mulder challenged.

Barron sighed heavily. "I hope you're not trying to interrogate me, Agent Mulder, because I am not the suspect."

Mulder leaned toward the detective. "You don't know anything about this case. Which is why you stuck Detective Ryan with it. Why don't you let her decide how to proceed?" Far from thanking Mulder for supporting her, Kelly glared at Mulder for dragging her into the spotlight.

"Detective Ryan *is* handling this case," Barron said with immense control. "She's done well, and I see no reason not to let her continue to prosecute it once the prisoner has been transferred." Kelly stepped closer to her supervisor and gave the two agents another fierce look.

"Whoa," Mulder said, and glared at Barron. "Transferred where?"

"To the city jail. In preparation for his arraignment."

Mulder's jaw tensed. "I don't think you appreciate this man's condition," Mulder insisted, "or the danger he poses—"

"And I don't think you have the authority

to tell me or anybody else in my unit how to do our job," Barron said, clearly skilled at ending conversations.

At that moment, Kelly stepped between the two angry men. "We can handle it from here, Agent Mulder," she said crisply. "We'll call you if there's anything more you can do."

Mulder narrowed his eyes at her. He wasn't finished, but Scully turned to him and said, "Come on, Mulder. Let's go."

Mulder grabbed Kelly's arm urgently. "Soft light," he hissed under his breath. "The man needs soft light."

Kelly gave him an even look, and he let go of her arm.

Mulder caught up with Scully quickly. "I hope you realize what you're doing," he said brusquely.

She turned to look at him. "What do you mean?"

"You're putting Detective Ryan's ambition ahead of all good sense on this case."

Scully stopped dead in the corridor, making

sure that no one could hear. "Ambition? She's just a woman trying to survive the boys' club, Mulder. And believe me, I know exactly how she feels."

Mulder felt his anger cool as Scully's temper flared. But his feelings about this case remained strong. "How she feels is one thing. The difference, Scully, is that you *never* put yourself ahead of the work. And that's exactly what Detective Ryan is doing."

Scully's anger suddenly deflated, and she felt at a loss for words. From Mulder, this was high praise indeed. She solemnly returned his steady regard. "The fact is," she said carefully, "we have no jurisdiction here. We were called in as a favor."

"And as a favor we just handed the A-bomb to the Boy Scouts."

"I'm sure all the necessary precautions will be taken." Even in her own ears the words sounded impotent and filled with doubt.

"And I'm sure the government gave Robert Oppenheimer a similar reassurance," Mulder countered. "The same government Dr. Banton is afraid of."

Scully shook her head incredulously. "You don't really believe that paranoia about 'brain suck,' do you?"

"The man is scared, Scully," he said urgently. "And not just of his own shadow."

"Mulder, as brilliant as Dr. Banton may be, he's also clearly delusional. He demonstrated just about every textbook indicator back there—"

Mulder interrupted her. "We've both seen the physical evidence, Scully."

"Look, I don't know how to explain it, but that's not our job. I don't know what else we can do."

Mulder sighed, and she could see—and share—his lingering frustration. He swung away from her and started down the hall.

"I think I know what to do," he said. His face was set with grim purpose as he walked away.

Scully could feel him shutting her out, and she didn't like it. She watched Mulder disappear around the corner, and it took every ounce of control not to chase after him. Sometimes she had to let him pursue his own demons, but it didn't make it any easier to let him go.

Chapter Nine

Emblazoned in the back of Mulder's mind, but unrecorded on this Earth, was the image of a tall, dark man who had no name—a man who, according to all public records, did not even exist. Mulder knew very well that there were covert government agencies, just as Dr. Banton had said, layered one behind another—some so far removed from the outside world that not even the FBI or the CIA knew they existed. The nameless man, whom Mulder had named X, was Mulder's contact with that secret government underworld. Mulder often suspected that the man was tied into the deepest core of government secrecy—or maybe he wasn't with the government at all. Yet somehow, he could always manage to fix the most dangerous of situations, and always had answers—even if he refused to share them with Mulder.

Mulder waited in the train station for less than an hour. When X approached through a side door, his hands were tucked in the pockets of his long black coat. He caught Mulder's attention with a piercing stare and then sauntered off to a dimly lit stairwell. Mulder followed, meeting him one flight down. X had chosen the spot well, as if he knew exactly where to go to get out of the view of the station's many security cameras.

"All you've given me is a name," said X. "Chester Banton."

"Dr. Chester Banton," corrected Mulder. "Do you know him?"

"No," answered X, "should I?" Somehow it surprised Mulder that his contact didn't know everything about Banton already. But then, maybe he was playing dumb. Like so many things about the man, it was just impossible to know.

"He's being held by the Richmond police in connection with several bizarre murders," explained Mulder. "He's a physicist, researching dark matter. He believes the government is out to get him."

"It's tax season. So do most Americans," said X, keeping a perfectly straight face.

"He believes his life is in danger."

"Is he a dangerous man?"

"He most definitely is," said Mulder, without a second thought. "A very dangerous man."

X took only a moment to consider this. "Where is he being held?" he asked.

"The Yaloff Psychiatric Hospital," Mulder answered. "But not for long."

X kept his eyes locked on Mulder. "I'm sorry I can't help you," he said coldly and decisively.

"Why?"

"The last time I helped you, I bloodied my fist and regrettably exposed my identity to associates of yours."

Now it was Mulder's turn to do some damage control. "Yes, I know. And you can trust them as you trust me. I promise you that." Mulder looked for some sort of change in the mysterious man's glare, but there was none—there never was.

"Dead men don't keep promises," X said. "Next time, the blood and regret could be yours." Mulder couldn't hold his gaze; he had to look away, if only for an instant. "I'm not at your beck and call, Agent Mulder," X chided. "I have nothing to gain and everything to lose by helping you."

Mulder opened his mouth to say something, to try to convince him, but thought better of it.

X spoke once more. "Promise me you won't contact me again unless it's absolutely necessary." And then, without waiting for an answer, he turned his back on Mulder and strode down the stairs and out the door into the darkness.

Chapter Ten

In the halls of Yaloff Psychiatric Hospital's Observation Ward, only one patient's room remained lit. The nurse on duty had just completed the early morning room check and was sitting behind her desk, finishing a pile of reports that were already days overdue. She thought she'd have the rest of the night to catch up on her work, but as luck would have it, the floor was suddenly immersed in darkness.

She sighed at the interruption. The nurse picked up the phone and dialed another extension. "Frank, are your lights on down there? Ours just went out."

Suddenly a hand clamped over the receiver. The startled nurse looked up but was blinded by the glare of a flashlight shined deliberately into her eyes. "Hi," said X's calm and deadly cold voice directly in front of her. "We're here to transfer Dr. Chester Banton." She tried to see the face behind the flashlight, but she could discern nothing beyond the fact that the man was tall and dark.

"I have orders that Dr. Banton is not to be transferred until tomorrow," said the nurse, trying to keep calm in the face of this unsettling situation.

"Due to the power outage, there's been a change in plans," said the tall man. He took the keys from her desk and strode off down the hall. In the receding beam of the flashlight, she could see two other men beside him, and they were rolling a gurney.

"Wait!" shouted the nurse. "No one's supposed to go down there!" But it was clear her warning meant nothing to these men, whoever they were.

Down the hall, X quickly found Dr. Banton's room and yanked the bolt, pulling the door open to let his operatives in.

"Quickly," he said.

He hadn't been entirely truthful with Mulder.

The fact was, he could help Mulder in this investigation—in a manner of speaking. Primarily because he knew exactly who Dr. Chester Banton was and what he was capable of. He had known long before Mulder, and his own operatives had been out looking for the man since he had disappeared.

Behind him the nurse came charging down the hall, and again he aimed his high-beam flashlight in her eyes, making certain that she did not see his face.

"Who *are* you?" she demanded. X chose not to respond. She was too insignificant to waste his breath on. In an instant she wheeled and ran down the hallway, presumably looking for help that wouldn't come until the job was done. He turned and looked inside the room. In nearly total darkness, his operatives slapped a heavy piece of duct tape over the complaining Dr. Banton's mouth and tied his hands together behind his back.

Just as they were trying to bind his feet, someone reconnected the emergency generator. Bright emergency lights came on, and

Dr. Banton, who had just been forced to his feet, suddenly cast a shadow.

X saw it all happen with his own eyes, but it was still impossible to believe. Both of his operatives were caught instantly by the shadow. The two men disappeared in a flash of blue light, dissolving into black puddles burning into the linoleum floor, quickly hardening into solid ash. And Chester Banton, silenced by the strip of tape across his mouth, only stared at X with a gaze of utter contempt. Never taking his eyes off X, Banton stepped over the two piles of ash, his shadow moving along with him. X quickly backed away, stepping to the side. As Banton stepped out of the room, X pulled his gun. The hallway emergency lights cast Dr. Banton's shadow in X's direction again.

The deaths of X's two operatives—those had been accidents, just like all the others, but if Banton took another step forward toward the mysterious agent, it would be murder. X banked on the fact that Chester Banton was not a murderer, and slowly lowered his weapon. The second he did, Banton turned and ran, taking his deadly dark matter with him.

Kelly Ryan halted abruptly when she caught sight of Mulder and Scully heading toward her down the hall of the psychiatric hospital less than an hour later. Then she became aware of a uniformed policeman watching her and of the forensic team working busily around her. Refusing to let on that she was somehow involved with the two FBI agents, she hardened her face and brushed past Mulder and Scully without saying anything. Mulder's gaze followed her as she walked down the hallway and out the door.

"Mulder," Scully said. Mulder turned and saw Scully crouching over the charred remains that were burned into the floor of Chester Banton's softly lit cell. She stood and stepped carefully over the second scorch mark on the floor.

"What did you find out?" Mulder asked.

"Richmond PD had two officers outside

watching the entrance. They didn't see anyone enter."

"According to the floor nurse, there were three men—"

"Three?"

The agents regarded the two scorch marks on the ground. What had happened to the third man?

"The power was disconnected at a substation two blocks from here," Scully said thoughtfully. "Somebody posing as a city engineer."

Mulder slouched against the wall and stared down the brightly illuminated corridor. "Somebody who had access to Virginia Power blueprints, so they could take the hospital off the grid without affecting surrounding facilities."

Scully's eyebrows rose. "Somebody inside the government? Coming for Dr. Banton?"

"Just because you're paranoid doesn't mean they're not out to get you, Scully." Mulder gave her an ironic look, then turned his attention back to the crime scene. "My guess is they were unsuccessful here, and that Banton's back on the loose."

"That's what Detective Ryan thinks, too," Scully said.

"I just saw her leaving," Mulder offered tentatively. He wasn't sure if he should discuss Detective Ryan's mood with Scully. She seemed to be very protective of her former student.

"Kelly was in charge of Dr. Banton's transfer and arraignment this morning. So, she's in some pretty hot water."

"It was an appointment he was never meant to keep, Scully. C'mon. Let's go."

He headed away from the crime scene into the hallway. Scully had to trot to keep up with him. "Where are we going?"

He looked down the hall. "You heard what Dr. Banton said in there."

"He said a lot of things," Scully said stubbornly.

Mulder swung back to face her. "Put yourself in his head, Scully. The only reason he hasn't killed himself is because he's afraid his death will release the dark matter."

Mulder could feel time running out, but Scully tried to slow him down. "Wait a minute. That's still just a theory, and a wild one at that." She shifted uncomfortably—hating to stand in Mulder's way when he was obviously acting out of concern for Dr. Banton.

But Mulder agreed with her. "Whether or not Dr. Banton is telling the truth, he believes he is."

Scully's head jerked up, and Mulder could see that she finally understood where he was leading her. "And apparently whoever tried to take him last night also believes it's true," she said.

"All that he's been trying to do since the accident is try to control this thing. Now if he escaped he's going to go the one place where he thinks he can do that. We've got to get there first," Mulder said, walking away.

Chapter Eleven

Dim moonlight hit the venetian blinds and was sliced into diagonal strips splayed across the Polarity Magnetics simulation room. The mag-lev bullet train sat silently, along with all the other models, while around them their controlling computers hummed a low sleeping buzz.

Dr. Chester Banton had arrived twenty minutes earlier, and now heard footsteps coming down the hall toward the room. He pushed himself up beside the door. He had phoned, leaving desperate messages with Morris West and Christopher Davey—the only two colleagues he knew he could trust. But neither of them answered the phone in the middle of the night. He managed to get an answering machine for Chris, and that blasted hotel operator for Morris. He only hoped that this was one of them now, coming down the hall. He heard the footsteps stop; a door opened down the hall, then closed again, and the footsteps continued toward the simulation room. Banton wouldn't open the door until he was certain who it was. He could take no chances. The time was short, and there was no room for error. If it wasn't one of them, Banton knew he'd have to go through with this alone—but without a partner, there was no guaranteeing it would go according to plan.

Finally the door opened slowly and a hand came into view, reaching for the light switch beside the door. Banton could instantly see that it was Christopher Davey. Banton grabbed Davey's hand just before he could touch the light switch, and Davey flinched in surprise.

"Don't turn on the light, Chris," warned Banton. "Not unless you want to die."

Davey squinted, trying to see his friend, but Banton still kept himself hidden in shadow—for as long as the shadows weren't his own, Davey was safe.

"Chester, what's going on? The FBI is looking for you—where have you been?"

Banton shook his head. "There's no time to explain right now. Just come with me."

Banton leaned out of the room into the dim hallway. Davey had done what Banton had asked when he had left that phone message—he hadn't turned on any of the hallway lights. There were swatches of blue up and down the hall as moonlight cut through the blinds—but those patches of light could easily be avoided. Banton strode down the hallway, cutting a serpentine path, with Davey following in his shadowless wake as they headed toward the particle accelerator.

"What's this about, Chester?" Davey asked insistently. "You're acting crazy. Talk to me! You *have* to tell me what's going on."

Banton didn't slow his pace down the hall. "We found the dark matter, Chris—it's real. We *found* it!"

"What are you talking about?"

"Don't you understand?" snapped Banton, with no patience for a step-by-step explanation. "I'm *it*. It's in *me*."

Davey's blinking confusion started to fade as he put two and two together. "The accident?"

"Yes," said Banton. "It changed me—it *altered* me. And now there's something living in my shadow—some sort of antimaterial predator that consumes organic matter instantaneously."

Again, it was too much for Davey, and he shook his head. "I . . . I don't understand."

"You don't have to, Chris," Banton told him. "All you need to know is that they're coming for me, and we have to destroy this thing before they get here."

They rounded a corner and saw her just as they heard her voice: a small but determined woman standing directly in their path. "Police!" she shouted, raising her gun and pointing it directly at Banton's chest. "I'm placing you under arrest, Dr. Banton."

It only took a moment for Banton to recognize her. It was Detective Ryan—the policewoman who had interrogated him after agents Mulder and Scully had left the psychiatric hospital.

Banton stopped walking. Didn't this woman understand what she was up against? "A lot of people will die if you do this," he warned her.

"Step over to the wall!" She was unyielding in her demand. And she was also very much alone. No partner, no backup.

"I don't want to hurt you," Banton said. "I'm begging you, please—"

"Step against the wall! Now!"

Davey made no move to help or to hinder; he just stood there like a spectator, pushing his glasses farther up on his face. Banton turned to see that behind him an unblinded window let in the light of the rising sun. When he turned back to Detective Ryan, he could see his black shadow only inches from the tips of her feet.

It gave Banton pause . . .

There had been many accidents already. The ones before he understood what was happening—and the accidents that had come when people wouldn't heed his warnings.

Maybe that was the only way to solve this. He had no choice. He had to hurry before they found him.

"I'm sorry," he said. And with that, Dr. Chester Banton raised his right hand high above his head and watched as the shadow of that hand stretched toward the feet of Detective Kelly Ryan. "I'm so sorry," he said.

Ryan, not understanding, not knowing his power, kept her gun trained on him, not his shadow. Then the tip of his shadow-fingers touched her shoes, and the ambitious young detective simply dropped out of existence.

Her scream was so short, it was a mere yelp that echoed down the empty corridors. The blue sparking on the ground flashed and faded until it vanished, leaving only a patch of fused, blackened matter burned into the floor tiles.

Christopher Davey gaped in shock, but Banton wasted no time on it. "Let's go," he said, stepping over the pile of ash and heading again toward the particle accelerator.

Once in the accelerator control room, Banton went straight for the digital lock of the target room door. He quickly punched in the code, and when it blinked green, he spun the heavy silver wheel. The door unlatched with a clang and a hiss of air. Then he pulled with all his strength on the mighty door until it swung open. Only as he stood on the threshold of the room where he had suffered his horrible accident did he hesitate. Before him lay the great machine that took the shattered particles of creation and focused them into a single beam. He could still see the image of his *true* shadow, burned forever into the lead wall. His true shadow was dead—but his new shadow was very much alive. The only way to kill it, he knew, was to bombard himself with positive particles. The dark matter would die . . . and maybe he would die, too, the antiparticles of his shadow merging with his own flesh, canceling each other out. But he would have to accept that possibility. His life was a small price to pay to save the world from this thing.

"Chester!" shouted Davey behind him. It was Davey's voice that propelled Banton through the hatch into the lead-walled target room. Then Banton spared one last gaze at Chris Davey before pulling the door closed behind him.

"No matter what people say later, you're doing the right thing, Chris." The door closed with a heavy thud, and Banton peered out through a double-paned four-inch round window in the door. A tiny porthole to the outside world. Banton could now see only half of Davey's face through that window. "Lock it up, Chris," ordered Banton.

Davey eyed him for a moment. Then, Banton heard the familiar beeping of the keypad, and the heavy clang as the locking mechanism engaged, sealing off one room from the other. Banton felt relief flow through him even as his fear spiked. "All right, Chris. Let's get the accelerator on-line."

But the expression on Davey's face didn't

seem right. It seemed a little too powerful. A little too . . . victorious. "I'm afraid I can't do that, Chester."

Banton pushed his face closer to the observation hole, to see if he could catch more of Davey's face. "You can do it, Chris!"

"I can," said Davey, with the slightest smile, "but I won't."

All at once it hit him. "No . . . no, Chris! Tell me you're not working for *them*."

But Davey's smile told all. "I wish I could—but the fact is I've been working with them from the beginning."

This was the worst part of Chester Banton's living nightmare—that he would be betrayed by a friend this close to killing the thing. He screamed and pounded on the door, but it was no use. That lock was designed to withstand everything short of a nuclear blast. "Davey, you lousy, stinking bastard!" He pounded the door again and again until he could feel the pain in his fists.

"Careful," jeered Davey. "Wouldn't want you to hurt yourself."

"I'll die before I let them use me!"

But Davey was as calm as could be, now that Banton was well trapped. "You're lightning in a bottle, Chester," he said. "We're not about to let you die."

He offered Chester a wide, gloating smile; then he disappeared from the peephole, leaving Chester to continue banging against the lead-lined door, with no hope of escape, and no hope of destroying the creature at his heels.

Christopher Davey strolled over to the computer console. He sat down comfortably in the rolling desk chair. It had all been remarkably easy. Banton had walked right into the trap. The hardest part for Davey had been pretending not to understand Banton's predicament—but he had to admit, when he'd seen that woman cop disintegrate before his eyes, he'd been truly astonished. He had heard what the dark matter was capable of, but to see it happen before his eyes ... it was like witnessing the hand of God. And to think he had been a part of creating that! The thought swelled his head.

He could see Banton on the video monitor, through its distorted fish-eye lens. Banton stood alone in the middle of the target room, looking up at the camera. "Chris, don't do this," he begged. "Listen to me, this is wrong!"

But Davey was done talking. At least to Banton. He picked up the phone and dialed by memory the number of his contact.

"You're making a terrible mistake," Banton continued to beg from the locked room, his voice shaky and weak.

"I've got him," Davey whispered into the phone. "He's not going anywhere until you pick him up."

He hung up and looked at the video screen again. Banton looked as small and helpless as a bacteria under a microscope. Who was the genius now?

Suddenly a splatter of blood hit the screen he was watching. Davey's eyes went dark, and he felt himself falling forward. There was only a brief instant of pain in the back of his head.

Davey never had the chance to realize what had happened to him, because he was dead before his face hit the desk.

Inside the target room, just a few feet away from the deadly accelerator, Chester Banton pounded on the door until he heard a faint sound. A high-pitched *Pfffft*, followed by the tinkle of breaking glass.

"Chris?" His fear rose to a sudden panic. "Chris, what's going on out there?" He waited for an answer, but none came. Not from Chris Davey.

Suddenly a face eclipsed the dim light of the small window—but it wasn't Chris. Through the hole a black man with a thick mustache scrutinized Banton with eyes that held such power and presence, Banton had to back away from the small window. He knew this man. He had passed up the chance to kill him in the hospital hallway just an hour ago. Now it was too late. Whatever this mysterious man was up to, Banton knew he was completely at his mercy.

Chapter Twelve

One hour later. There was a single car in the parking lot of Polarity Magnetics when Scully and Mulder arrived. Scully and Mulder knew it belonged to Kelly Ryan. Scully turned to Mulder with eyes that spoke volumes.

"We're not the first ones here, Mulder. That's Detective Ryan's car," said Scully.

They drew their weapons as they hurried toward the building. "I was afraid of this," Mulder said as they quickened their pace.

They stormed the stairs and burst out onto the second floor, where the door to Polarity Magnetics was ajar. Inside the halls of the high-tech facility all was dim and quiet. They hurried down the hall, guns at the ready, not daring to speak to each other. Then, as they rounded a corner, they came upon a pile of black ash near an unshuttered window. The moonlight cast their shadows across the patch of ash. Scully took a moment to kneel down over the spot.

"We don't know it's her," Mulder said. But Scully knew better. Kelly had come here to arrest Banton. Who else could it be? As they had been so many times in this case, their efforts were too little, too late.

Suddenly a strange droning sound began to pulsate in their ears. It rattled through them and shook the floor. The crumbling ash that had been Kelly Ryan began to resonate and vibrate with the sound.

Scully got to her feet, knowing she couldn't grieve for Kelly now. "What's that noise?" It was unfamiliar. Strange—like a spaceship powering up for takeoff. Then she realized what it was, at the exact same moment Mulder did.

"The accelerator!"

They both took off down the hall.

The door to the accelerator control room was open, but no one was at the computer terminal. A bright, white light was strobing in the target room—they could see it through the small round window in the lead door. On the video screen of the computer, the situation was clear. A man sat unconscious in the chair, bombarded by wave after wave of subatomic particles. The beam hit him, turning him blinding white with each strobe and leaving him darker and darker after each blast of light, until there was nothing left of him but the darkness. He was gone, the chair was gone, and nothing remained but his shadow burned into the wall. Then the flashes slowed, the accelerator powered down, and the room stopped vibrating.

Mulder and Scully tried to pull open the target room door, but it was locked, and they didn't know the code to punch into the keypad. Through the small window they could see two shadows now: the first one, made by Banton when he first released the dark matter into the world, and the second one, made when he left it.

"He must have turned on the accelerator

and sealed himself in," Scully postulated, but Mulder shook his head.

"It couldn't be. This door's locked from the outside, Scully." He pounded his hand against the door.

That one threw Scully for a loop. "By whom?" she asked.

But Mulder had no answer—at least none that he would share.

In the darkest corner of the seediest industrial area of Richmond sat a sports arena that had been abandoned for years. Only rats had business there. Rats, and Agent Fox Mulder. He stormed across the huge space filled with predawn fog. Someone was supposed to meet him here, but he wasn't in any of the open spaces. Mulder didn't expect he would be. Mulder walked past a stone wall, noticing how his shadow played sharp and rigid against the cold cinder block surface. Then, out of nowhere, there was a second shadow next to his.

"Agent Mulder!"

He spun to see the mysterious X, hands in

the pockets of his raincoat. In control of the situation. Always in control.

"I thought you agreed not to contact me again about Dr. Banton," said the covert agent.

Mulder got right to the point. "You lied to me," he said.

"About what?"

"About Chester Banton!" Mulder didn't hold back his anger. His voice was loud, and he didn't care if it echoed through the arena. "You knew who he was, and you used me to lead you to him."

"It was *you* who contacted *me*, Agent Mulder."

"I won't be your stalking horse—or the government's," Mulder said.

X took a breath, slowly and evenly. "You seem to be mistaken about the amount of control you exercise over this arrangement."

The calm in X's voice only made Mulder angrier. *"You killed Dr. Banton!"*

X paused, but only for an instant. "Have you lost your mind?"

"The nurse at the hospital identified you,"

shouted Mulder. "A young detective is dead because of you. *Who do you answer to?*"

X took a step forward. The expression on his face never changed, but his eyes—it was as if he could kill Mulder with a single withering look. "Despite my loyalty to my predecessor," he said, "I've never made you any promises."

Mulder returned his sharp look. This time it was his turn to get in X's face, speaking quietly through clenched teeth.

"All right, then, make me this promise: Promise me that this will be our last meeting. We're finished." Then Mulder turned to walk off, refusing to give his mysterious contact anything but his back.

"You're choosing a dangerous time to go it alone, Agent Mulder," X said, as Mulder left. Mulder could sense for the first time that X was losing that tight control he had wielded since their very first meeting. Mulder didn't respond; he just kept walking. Until X said something that Mulder could not walk away from.

"I didn't kill him, Mulder."

Mulder turned and saw the nameless agent standing in shadows, but there was enough light on his face to see that he was offering a truce. A bit of information that he probably didn't want to give. Chester Banton was still alive. X turned and sauntered away—and although X had had the last word, Mulder couldn't help feeling that in some small way, he had still won.

Chapter Thirteen

A warm front had finally settled in, heralding spring in Richmond, and so Kelly Ryan's memorial service was not the black-umbrella, windblown affair that it could have been. Instead it was bright and sunny. Which in its own way was terrible, too.

Scully stayed inconspicuously in the background as the priest said kind and compassionate words to grieving friends and relatives. Most of the Richmond Police Department stood at attention in rows behind the grave. A news crew taped for the five-o'clock news, preparing a story about a young policewoman who had fallen in the line of duty. It was just the kind of heart-wrenching story that made good news. But neither the media nor the family would ever know the true disposition of Kelly Ryan's body, and how it came to be just a pile of black ash.

When the service was over, Scully lingered for a few moments. She walked around the endless arrangements of flowers, thinking she might say something to Kelly's grieving parents. But she was intensely relieved when they left before she could catch them. What would she have said to them? Instead she knelt by the grave and looked at the tombstone which marked Kelly's short life.

Then she turned and strode over to Mulder, who had just arrived and was waiting for her.

"I don't know how to feel about this," she confided in him. "Kelly was my student, and she came to me for help. . . ."

"I know it must be hard," said Mulder, from behind a pair of dark glasses. Somehow his compassion felt distant, as if something else was on his mind.

Scully glanced back at the grave and again played the scene over in her mind: her own imaginary picture of Kelly's last moment, the moment that she dropped out of existence.

How horrible it must have been for her. "This never should have happened," Scully said.

"I'm sorry I'm late," said Mulder, changing the subject. "I got hung up at the Richmond PD."

"Doing what?"

Mulder glanced around to make sure they were unobserved. "A missing persons report was filed this morning by a Dr. Morris West. He's a physicist affiliated with Polarity Magnetics."

Scully had thought this case was over. Why was Mulder bringing it back now? "I'm not sure I'm following you."

"The missing person," Mulder explained, "is Dr. Christopher Davey. He hasn't been seen or heard from since Banton disappeared."

"Do they have any leads?"

"No. None," said Mulder.

But Scully knew Mulder's tone of voice and his body language well enough to have insight into what he was thinking. Sometimes such insight was fortunate, other times unfortunate. "But you know, don't you?" she prompted.

"What if it wasn't Banton we saw in the particle accelerator, Scully? What if he wasn't the one who was disintegrated?"

Scully took a sharp breath. "But if Banton's not dead, then where is he?"

Mulder didn't even pretend to have an answer to that one. Scully's question was met with silence, and she knew that this was one case that would never be closed.

Elsewhere, in a top secret government installation, the man known only as X strode down a hall toward a heavy vault door. Standing in front of the heavy door, a scientist peered in through a small square of leaded glass, squinting against the slow strobing light within the small room. He took notes, studied the computer console before him, and shook his head in amazement.

X studied the spikes and dips racing past on the computer screen. "Is the data making sense?" he asked.

"Not yet," answered the scientist. "It's like we have to create a whole new branch of physics just to deal with this. We'll need some top minds."

X threw an unkind gaze at the scientist. "I thought you were the top mind."

The scientist shrugged. "Maybe. But Dr. Davey really would have been helpful to us. I have a feeling we'll be studying this man for a long, long time."

Beyond the glass, in the tiny lead-lined room, sat Chester Banton. His arms and legs were strapped to a hard steel chair. Electrodes had been attached to his skull, accessing every part of his brain, and wires extended down his arms and legs, measuring every physical reaction. In front of him sat the business end of a particle accelerator, which bombarded him every three seconds with tiny quantities of subatomic particles like some sort of high-tech water torture. Meanwhile, behind him, against a huge photoelectric cell, his shadow grew blacker and blacker with each pulse.

Banton stared into the machine but didn't see anything. He had long since been blinded by the neutrinos bombarding his retina ...

but he could still hear. He heard the whispered conversations outside the door, and he heard the awful rhythmic groan of the machine, sounding like the dark breathing of a quantum beast. As he sat there flinching and twitching against a steel bar that held his head in place, a single tear rolled down his face, for now he felt the last remnants of his mind slipping away from him forever...

... as if the machine were sucking away his brain, particle, by particle, by particle...

EASTON ROYCE is a pseudonym for a well-known award-winning children's book author.

**Read the next book in the
X-Files Young Adult series:**

**The X-Files #11: Howlers
by Everett Owens**

Mary didn't hear the footsteps behind her, but she felt a sharp prick in her shoulder as a form brushed by her.

"Ow! Hey, you jerk!" she snapped, but the yellow-clad figure kept walking and didn't look back.

She stood there wondering why the person didn't turn around. Reaching back to the spot where she'd felt the prick, she was surprised to see a dot of blood on her hand. Then dizziness hit with a confusing suddenness. Mary's face lost its color, and she began to blink rapidly. She wanted someone to tell her what was happening, but the only word she was able to get out of her mouth was "What . . ."

Lurching straight through a mud puddle,

she stumbled toward Billy's car. As she approached, she could see the back of Billy's head through the rear windshield. Smoke from his cigarette wafted out of the crack in the driver's side window.

"Billy! Someone did something to me," Mary managed.

Somewhere in the back of her mind, it occurred to Mary that she'd probably been drugged. She would be safe, she decided, if she could just make it to the car. Sheer willpower got her there, but by the time she reached the VW, she had to lean on it to keep from falling.

Why wasn't Billy turning around? Why couldn't he hear her?